The Case of the Red Bicycle

by Chin Moy
illustrated by Debby Fisher

Harcourt

Orlando Boston Dallas Chicago San Diego

Visit The Learning Site!

www.harcourtschool.com

Brrring! Brrring!

Sam loved his new bicycle. He finally learned how to ride it. He did not fall off anymore.

Sam's bicycle was red. It was as red as the apples he ate after school. Sam wore a blue helmet when he rode his bike.

Up and down the sidewalk he rode. Sam pushed down on the pedals. He held onto the handlebars. The tires went around and around.

Sam's bike had a silver bell. It shined in the sunlight. Brrring! Brrring! Sam loved to ring the bell at everyone.

Brrring! Brrring! "Clear the way!" the bell said. "Watch out!" The bell made a pleasant sound.

Everyone smiled at Sam. Everyone moved out of the way when they heard the bell. Sam loved to ride his bike and ring the bell.

"Here comes that kid again," Cliff said to himself.

Brrring! "Move out of the way!" Sam yelled. The bicycle was coming closer to Cliff. But Cliff stayed on the sidewalk. Sam was getting closer and closer to Cliff.

Brrring! went the bell. "Watch out! Move out of the way!"

Cliff jumped out of the way. He heard the tires swoosh by him. He didn't like that kid. He didn't like that bicycle. He didn't like this new place.

Cliff was new in the neighborhood. His family had just moved there. His mother had a new job.

Cliff was learning about his neighborhood. All the houses looked the same. All the streets were very long. There was no noise. Everything was quiet except for that bicycle.

"This place is not like the city," Cliff thought. In the city, Cliff could ride on a big bus. "There are no buses here," Cliff said to himself.

Sam pedaled around the corner. He rode by the only blue house on the street. Sam knew that a new family had just moved in. There were two kids in the family.

The blue house looked very quiet. No one played in the yard. No car was parked in the driveway. There were no lights on in the house. It looked like no one was home.

"Oh, well," thought Sam. "I'll come back later." He turned the handlebars and rode back the other way.

"Come on, Racer," Sam said to his bike.

Sometimes Sam pretended his bicycle was a racehorse. The handlebars became the horse's mane. The pedals became stirrups for Sam's feet.

Sam pushed the pedals harder and harder. The tires went around and around. Sam pretended to see a finish line at the end of the block.

"Come on, Racer. Come on!" Sam said. "Faster, faster!"

Cliff heard the bell again. Brrring! Brrring! That kid was coming back. This time Cliff did not move. "Let him go around me," Cliff thought.

Brrring! "Move out of the way! Move out of the way!"

"Not this time," thought Cliff. "I'm not moving."

The red bicycle came closer to Cliff. Its tires were spinning fast. But Cliff just stood there. He would not move.

"Move out of the way!" Brrring!

One of the tires ran over Cliff's foot. Sam turned the bicycle off the sidewalk. He stopped the bike.

"Are you okay?" Sam asked Cliff. Cliff moved his foot. It looked okay, but it hurt!

"Ow!" Cliff cried. "My foot really hurts!" Cliff took off his shoe and sock. His foot was turning black and blue.

Sam looked at Cliff's foot. It was starting to swell.

"You did this," Cliff said.

"I did not," said Sam. "You wouldn't move off the sidewalk."

"I'm going home," yelled Cliff. "My foot hurts." Cliff tried to walk, but his foot hurt too much.

"I can't walk. My foot hurts." Cliff sat down on the curb. Cliff was almost crying. Sam suddenly felt sorry for him.

Sam thought for a minute. "Do you want me to go get someone?" Sam said. Then he had an idea. "Do you want to ride my bike to my house? It is closer. Riding the bike might hurt less than walking."

Cliff didn't want to go to Sam's house. He didn't want to ride the bicycle. Cliff didn't want to tell his secret. Cliff did not know how to ride a bicycle. He grew up in the city. It was too dangerous to ride there.

"Your bike is too small for me. Go home and get somebody," said Cliff.

When Sam looked down at his bicycle, he saw that the chain had come off. He put down the kickstand.

"I'll watch your bike," said Cliff.

"Okay," Sam said. "I'll be back."

Cliff sat on the curb for a very long time. He felt lonely. There was no one around. He didn't like this place. What was taking the boy so long?

Finally, a car drove up. Inside were a man and a boy. "There's the bike, Mike," the man said. The boy named Mike got out of the car.

"I'm watching this bike," Cliff said.

"That's okay," said Mike. "You don't have to watch it anymore."

Mike lifted up the kickstand. He put the bike in the trunk of the car. Cliff watched the car drive away.

Suddenly Cliff was worried. "Who took the bicycle away?" he asked himself. "I don't know those people."

Cliff got nervous. "Maybe the boy was a thief! Mike the thief. Maybe I let Mike the thief steal that boy's bicycle. Oh, no!" Cliff thought.

In the city, Cliff would have known what to do. In this place, he had no idea what to do next.

Cliff thought very hard. "The boy on the red bicycle never told me his name. I never told him my name."

Then Cliff heard a car coming. Maybe Mike the thief was coming back! Then he remembered the boy who had gone to get help. What would he do when he found out his bike had been stolen?

The car was coming closer and closer. Cliff saw that it was his mother's van. She pulled up next to him and rolled down the window. "Cliff," she said. "What are you doing?" Cliff's little sister Carole was in the back seat.

"I hurt my foot. I couldn't walk home!" Cliff said.

Cliff's mom helped him into the van. He was happy to finally see someone he knew.

"I was worried," Cliff's mother said. "You were gone for a very long time."

"I'm sorry," Cliff said. He was not going to tell his mother about the bicycle.

"Carole and I went shopping," Cliff's mother said. "Look in the back."

Cliff turned around. He saw two bicycles in the back of the van. A small purple bike was for his little sister. A bigger black bike was for Cliff.

"You'll learn to ride in no time," said his mother. "I'll help you."

Cliff smiled a little. "Thanks, Mom. That's great." Cliff's mother smiled, too.

The phone was ringing as Cliff, Carole, and their mother walked in the door. Cliff's mother answered the phone. "Hello?" she said.

Then she handed the phone to Cliff. "It's for you," she said.

"Hello?" said Cliff.

"Thanks for watching my bike," the voice said. It was the boy from earlier that day. "My name is Sam," the boy said.

Sam explained that his older brother and their father took the bike home. Cliff felt relieved. The mystery was solved! Sam's brother Mike was not a thief after all!

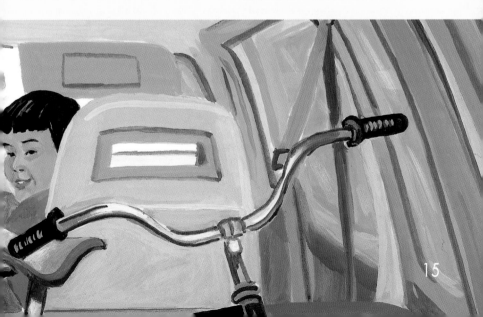

"How's your foot?" Sam asked.

"It still hurts a little," Cliff said. "But guess what? My mom bought me a new bicycle. She is going to show me how to ride. Maybe when my foot feels better, we can ride our bikes together. But I will have to practice first."

"It's a deal," Sam said to Cliff. "I will also have to practice, too, so I don't run over any more feet."

The two boys laughed. Both Cliff and Sam were glad that they had made a new friend.